Lulu the Big Little Chick

PAULETTE BOGAN

BLOOMSBURY

LONDON BERLIN NEW YORK

Bloomsbury Publishing, London, Berlin and New York

First published in Great Britain in 2009 by Bloomsbury Publishing Plc
36 Soho Square, London, W1D 3QY

First published in the USA in 2009 by Bloomsbury USA Children's Books
175 Fifth Avenue, New York, NY 10010

Text and illustrations copyright © by Paulette Bogan 2009
The moral right of the author/illustrator has been asserted

A CIP catalogue record of this book is available from the British Library

ISBN 978 1 4088 0202 1

Printed in China

1 3 5 7 9 10 8 6 4 2

All papers used by Bloomsbury Publishing are natural, recyclable products made from
wood grown in well-managed forests. The manufacturing processes conform to the
environmental regulations of the country of origin

www.bloomsbury.com/childrens

To my big little chicks,
Soph, Rach, and Lulu

Lulu was tired of being the littlest chick on the farm. She was too little to lay eggs. She was too little to climb the big fence. She was too little to play in the field of corn.

But when Mummy said, "Lulu, you are too little to go very far from me . . ."

. . . Lulu said, "NO. I am big and I am going far, far away."

"I see," said Mummy slowly. "So you are going far, far away?"

"Yes," said Lulu. "Right now."

"OK," said Mummy. "Goodbye, Lulu."

And Lulu marched out of the barn door.

"OINK, OINK. Where are you heading, little miss?" snorted Mrs Pig.

"I am going far, far away," said Lulu.

Splat. Lulu was covered with mud. "Sorry," giggled the piglet. "You're so little, I didn't see you!"

"This is not far, far away enough," said Lulu.

Mummy called out, "Do you need help getting clean, Lulu?"

"NO," said Lulu. "I am going far, far away, by myself."

"OK," Mummy said. "Goodbye, Lulu."

"This looks like far, far away," Lulu said, stepping into the sheep pen.

"BAA, BAA," said the sheep. "Watch out, little one. We almost squashed you!"

"This is not far, far away, anyway. Goodbye, sheep.
Goodbye, Mummy!" Lulu shouted. "I am really going
this time."

"I know," Mummy called. "You are going far, far
away. Goodbye, Lulu."

"Far, far away, here I come," said Lulu.

"NEIGH," said the horse. "I almost stepped on you!
Where do you think you are going, little chick?"

Lulu looked up and up and up. "Far, far away?" she whispered.

"You are too little to go far, far away," the horse neighed.

Lulu hurried away . . . straight into the biggest cow she had ever seen.

"MOO, I almost chewed you up with this tasty grass," said the cow. "What are you doing here, little lady?"

Lulu answered in a very small voice, "I am going far, far away?"

"HA," said the cow. "You are too little to go far, far away!"

Lulu got up and ran as fast and as far as she could. She did not see the pigs or the sheep or the horse or that big cow . . . or Mummy. Lulu gulped and said in a very tiny voice, "Uh-oh, I think I am far, far away now."

Then there was a terrible sound: CAW, CAW, CAW! A huge creature Lulu had never seen before was flying right over her head. Lulu could not move.

She whispered to herself, "I am a big chick, I am a big chick, I am . . . LITTLE!"

She closed her eyes as the sound came closer and closer. And then . . .

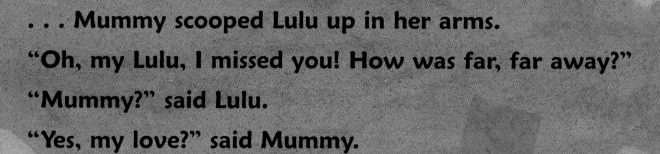

. . . Mummy scooped Lulu up in her arms.

"Oh, my Lulu, I missed you! How was far, far away?"

"Mummy?" said Lulu.

"Yes, my love?" said Mummy.

"Mummy, next time I go far, far away, I think I will take you with me."